# About Love

# Three Stories

by Anton Chekhov

# ABOUT LOVE

## 3 STORIES BY ANTON CHEKHOV

**TRANSLATED BY DAVID HELWIG**
**DESIGNED & DECORATED BY SETH**

BIBLIOASIS
2012

# 1

# A Man in a Shell

Ivan Ivanych & Burkin

ust at the edge of the village of Mironositskoe, in a shed belonging to Prokofy, the village elder, some hunters who had been kept late were settling themselves for the night. There were just two of them, a veterinarian, Ivan Ivanych, and Burkin, a high school teacher. Ivan Ivanych had a rather strange hyphenated family name – Chimsha-Himalaiski – which didn't suit him at all, and the whole province called him by his given name and patronymic; he lived close to the city on a farm that raised horses and had come hunting to get a breath of clean air. Burkin, the high school teacher, spent every summer as the guest of Count P. and had been on his own in this region for a while now.

They weren't asleep. Ivan Ivanych, a tall, lean old man with long whiskers, sat outside by the doorway and smoked a pipe; the moon cast its light on him. Burkin lay inside on the hay; he could not be seen in the darkness.

They were telling all sorts of stories. They got to talking about how the elder's wife, Mavra, a healthy woman and no fool, had never in her whole life gone beyond her native village, had never seen a city or a railroad, and for the last ten years just sat by the stove and never went out into the street except at night.

"How very strange that is!" Burkin said. "People of a solitary nature, who try to withdraw into a shell, without a bit of light, like a hermit crab or a snail. It could be that this atavistic phenomenon goes back to a time when our ancestors were not yet social creatures and lived alone, each in his own lair, or it could be that this is simply one of the varieties of human character – who knows? I'm not a scientist and it's not my business to deal with these questions; I just want to say that the occurrence of people like Mavra is not uncommon. Not at all. Not to look far from home, two months ago there was a death among us in the city, a certain Belikov, a teacher of Greek and a friend of mine. You've heard all about him, of course. He was conspicuous because he'd always go out, even in fine weather, in galoshes and with an umbrella, and without fail wearing a warmly lined overcoat. And his umbrella was in an umbrella case, and his watch in a watch case of grey chamois, and when he took out his penknife to sharpen his pencil, the knife was in a little case, and even his face seemed to be encased because he always concealed it in a high collar. He wore dark glasses, a sweater, stuffed his ears with cotton wool, and when he sat in a cab, he wanted the

13

top up. In a word, the man showed a constant and insuperable yearning to enclose himself inside a shell, to wrap himself up you might say in a way that would isolate him, protect him from external influences. Reality irritated him, frightened him, kept him in a state of constant alarm, and it may have been out of his timidity, his aversion to the present, that he always praised the past – and as it never was; the ancient languages he taught were in essence more galoshes and umbrellas in which he hid from the reality of life.

'Oh how sonorous, how heartfelt is the Greek language,' he'd say with a sweet expression, and as if in proof of his words he'd screw up his eyes and lifting his finger he'd articulate – '*Anthropos.*'

And Belikov tried to contain and control his very thoughts. For him the only comprehensible items in newspapers and circulars were those that forbid something. When some document circulated forbidding schoolchildren to go out in the street after nine in the evening or some item denounced carnal love, that was intelligible to him, definite; it was forbidden, basta! But any permission or authorization always concealed some dubious element, something shadowy and unspoken. When the city permitted a dramatic society or a reading room or a tea room he would rock his head back and forth and say softly, 'Of course that's so, and all very fine, but nothing can come of it.'

Any kind of disruption, evasion, digression from the rules led him into despondency, although it might seem to have nothing to do with him. If one of his comrades was late for a church service or if some schoolboy trick reached his ears, or if he saw a lady teacher with some officers late in the evening, he was very upset and told everyone – whatever might come of it. At the teachers' councils, he oppressed us with his prudence, his mistrustfulness and his tidy all-encompassing judgments about the young people, the students, boys and girls –

Look how they behave badly, making a lot of noise in class – and as if they didn't understand the rules, oh as if it didn't matter – and if Petrov was excluded from the second class and Yegorov from the fourth, it would be a very good thing. And then? What with his sighs, his whining, his dark eyes in his pale little face, you know, a little face like a weasel's, he wore us down, and we gave in, reduced Petrov's marks for behaviour and Yegorov's, made them sit apart from the others, and in the end we took Petrov and Yegorov and suspended them both. He had a strange habit of coming into our apartments. He'd arrive at a teacher's place and sit in silence, as if he was spying out something. He'd sit like that for a while in silence and the next minute he'd leave. He called it 'encouraging good relations among his colleagues,' and it was obviously hard for him to come in and sit there, and he came only because he considered it his duty as a colleague. We teachers were afraid of him. Even the principal was frightened. Just imagine our teachers, thoughtful people, profoundly decent, brought up on Turgenev and Shchedrin, and yet this man – going about in galoshes and with an umbrella – held the entire school in his grip for all of fifteen years. Did I say the school? The whole town. Our ladies didn't arrange performances in their homes on the Sabbath; they were afraid he would hear about it, and in his presence the clergy were ashamed to eat meat and play cards. Under the influence of people like Belikov, over the last ten or fifteen years people in our town became afraid of everything. Afraid to speak aloud, to send letters, to visit, to read books, afraid to help the poor, to teach reading and writing . . ."

Ivan Ivanych, searching for something to say, coughed, gave a puff on his pipe, stared at the moon and only then said in a measured voice: "Yes, intellectuals, decent people, they read Shchedrin and Turgenev, and others read H.T. Buckle and so on, but look how they take orders and suffer . . . That's just how it is."

"Belikov lived in the same building as I did" – Burkin continued – "on the same floor, one door facing the other, and we often saw each other. I knew about his domestic life. At home it was the same story: dressing gown, nightcap, shutters, bolts, a whole list of all the prohibitions and restrictions – oh, just in case something might happen. Fasting food didn't agree with him, but with animal flesh forbidden, lest it be said that Belikov didn't observe the fasts, he ate pike in butter – not the usual fasting food, but you couldn't say it was meat. He didn't keep a servant girl out of fear for his reputation, but he kept a cook, Aphanasy, an old man of sixty, drunk and half-demented, who at one time had served as a military orderly, and who knew how to dish up this and that. This Aphanasy usually stood by the door crossing his arms and always muttering the same thing, with deep sighs.

'A lot of *them* got it today.'

Belikov's bedroom was very small, not much more than a box and a cot with curtains. Lying down to sleep he pulled the covers over his head; it was hot, stifling, the wind rattled the closed doors, there was a howling in the stove; deep sighs were heard from the kitchen . . .

And beneath his blanket he was afraid. He was frightened that something might happen to him, that Aphanasy might murder him, that thieves might get in, and late in the night he'd have anxious dreams, and in the morning when we walked to the school together, he was on edge, pale, and it was evident that the bustling school he was going to was frightening and repulsive to his whole being, and that to walk along beside me was distressing to a person of his solitary nature.

'They've been making a lot of noise in our classrooms,' he said, as if trying to find an explanation for his dark mood. 'I've never heard anything like it.'

And this teacher of Greek, this man in a shell, can you imagine that he almost got married?"

Ivan Ivanych took a quick look in the shed and said, "You're joking."

"Yes, he nearly got married, however strange that may be. We were assigned a new history and geography teacher, a certain Mikhail Savvich Kovalenko, from the Ukraine. He arrived, not on his own, but with his sister Varenka. He was young, tall, swarthy, with enormous hands, and you knew just to look at him that he spoke in a bass voice, and in fact his voice was just like the sound out of a barrel – *boom, boom, boom.* And she was no longer young, thirty years old, but she was tall, well-proportioned, dark brows, red cheeks – in a word, not some dainty miss but a real jam tart, lively and adept, and she sang all the Little Russian romances and laughed out loud. At the drop of a hat she burst into full-throated laughter – *ha-ha-ha.* The first thing I remember as we grew familiar with the

Kovalenkos took place on the principal's name day. In the midst of those stern, so-very-boring teachers who dutifully attended the name day, we all of us together observed a new Aphrodite rise up from the foam: she walked about with her hands on her hips, laughed, sang, danced . . . She sang with feeling 'The Winds Whirl,' and then another romance and another, and she charmed us all, every one, even Belikov. He sat next to her, and smiling sweetly he said, 'The Little Russian language – in its delicacy and pleasant sonority – resembles ancient Greek.'

This pleased her, and she began to talk to him seriously and with feeling about how she had a farm in the district of Gadyachsko and on this farm lived her Mum, and there were such pears, such melons, such pubs – in the Ukraine they called the pumpkins pubs, and the pubs pothouses – and they cooked borscht with tomatoes and eggplant, 'so delicious, so delicious that it was simply . . . scary!'

We listened and we listened, and a thought came to all of us at once.

'It would be a good thing for them to marry,' the headmistress said to me quietly.

For some reason, we had all been reminded that our Belikov was unmarried, and at that moment it seemed strange to us that up till now we somehow hadn't exactly noticed, had entirely lost sight of such an important detail about his life. How did he generally regard women, had he made his own decision about this vital question? Up till now this didn't interest us at all; it may be that we didn't even allow ourselves to consider whether this man who went about in galoshes in all weathers and slept behind curtains might fall in love.

'He's well past forty now, and she's thirty . . .' the headmistress said, explaining what was in her mind. 'It seems to me she might accept him.'

Just what didn't occur to us in the provinces out of our boredom? So many redundancies, absurdities. And this one, though it didn't quite come about, seemed as if it should. But why did the lot of us feel the need to marry off this Belikov, whom we couldn't even imagine married? The headmistress, the inspector, and all our lady teachers grew animated, even grew better-looking, as if all together they had caught sight of a purpose in life. The headmistress rented a box in the theatre, and we kept an eye out – in the box sat Varenka with oh such a fan – beaming, happy, and beside her sat Belikov, small, doubled-up, as if he'd been dragged out of his house with pincers. I gave an evening party, and the ladies demanded that I invite – and without fail – both Belikov and Varenka. In a word, the machinery set to work. It turned out that Varenka was not unwilling to marry. Her life with her brother was not all that happy; the only thing we knew was that they argued all day long and abused each other. Here's a scene for you: Kovalenko goes out into the street, a tall, lanky fellow with an embroidered shirt, his hair

falling on his forehead out of his folding cap, a parcel of books in one hand, in the other a thick, knotty walking stick. Behind him comes his sister, also with some books.

'Well, then I say you didn't read it, Mikhailik,' she argues loudly. 'I swear you didn't read it at all.'

'And I tell you that I read it,' Kovalenko cries out, thumping his stick on the sidewalk.

'Oh my God, Michnik! You get so angry about it, and we're just having a principled discussion.'

'I told you I read it,' Kovalenko cries out even louder.

And at home whenever there was a visitor there was a squabble. Really, a life like that must have left her bored, wishing for a home of her own – yes, and there was age to consider. Living as she did would never work out; you'd want to marry anyone, even that teacher of Greek. All they talked about, the majority of our young ladies, was whether or not she'd marry him.

Whether that was to be or not, Varenka showed our Belikov obvious good will.

And Belikov? He visited Kovalenko just as he did the rest of us. He arrived and sat in silence. He was silent and Varenka sang to him 'The Wind Whirls' or glanced at him thoughtfully with her dark eyes, or suddenly laughed out loud.

'Ha-ha-ha.'

In matters of the heart, and especially when it comes to marriage, suggestion plays a large role. Everyone – gentlemen and ladies – assured Belikov that he was ready to marry, that marriage was the one thing left in life for him; we all congratulated him, recited with self-important faces our various commonplaces – that marriage was a serious step, for example – and besides, Varenka was not a bad or uninteresting choice for him; she was the daughter of a Councillor of State and understood farming, and most of all she was the first woman who had taken to him with warmth and affection.

His head was turned, and he actually decided he must marry her."

"And that would be the end of his galoshes and umbrella," remarked Ivan Ivanych.

"But you know it turned out to be impossible. He had furnished his place with a portrait of Varenka, which sat on a table, and he constantly came to me and spoke about Varenka, about domestic life, and of how marriage was a serious step; often he was at Kovalenko's, but his way of life didn't change a bit. Quite the reverse, the decision to marry had a troubling effect on him somehow, he lost weight, grew pale, and it seemed he sank deeper into his shell.

'I like Varvara Savvishna,' he said to me with a feeble, wry little smile – 'and I know everyone must marry, but . . . all this, you know, is happening so suddenly . . . I need to think.'

'What is there to think about?' I say to him. 'Marry and that's it.'

'No, marriage – it's a serious step, it's necessary first of all to examine one's future duties, responsibilities, compatibility . . . so that things don't come out later on. It worries me, so that I'm not sleeping at all. And to tell the truth, I'm frightened: at her place with her brother I think strange thoughts; they argue, don't you know, so strangely somehow, and their manner is so forward. You get married, and the next thing you know everyone's talking about you.'

He made no proposal, everything was put off, to the great disappointment of the headmistress and all our ladies; he weighed up all his future duties and responsibilities, and meanwhile almost every day he went for a stroll with Varenka – perhaps he thought it was required in this situation – and he came to my place to discuss his domestic life. In all likelihood he would in the end have made a proposal, and there would have occurred another of those unnecessary, foolish marriages which take place among us in thousands, out of tedium or for no reason at all, if suddenly there hadn't occurred a *kolosalische Scandal*. It has to be said that

Varenka's brother, Kovalenko, had conceived a dislike for Belikov from the very first day of meeting him, and by now he couldn't stand him.

'I don't understand,' he said to us, shrugging his shoulders. 'I don't understand how you can stand this informer, this loathsome bug. Oh gentlemen, how can you all live like this? The atmosphere around you is suffocating, foul. Really, are you pedagogues, teachers? You're servile. Yours is no temple of knowledge, but a worship of authority, and it stinks like a police cell. No, brothers, I'm here with you for a little while, then I'm off to the farm to catch crayfish, back where they laugh at learning. I'm going away, and you can stay here with your Judas, brooding on your sins.'

Or he'd laugh, laugh in a deep bass voice until tears came to his eyes and his voice grew thin and scratchy, and he'd ask me, his hands spread: 'What's he sit at my place for? What's he need? Sitting and staring.'

He even gave Belikov a nickname, 'the damned little spider.' Obviously we avoided mentioning to him that his sister Varenka was keeping company with the 'damned spider.' When one day the headmistress dropped a hint that it would be a fine thing to settle his sister permanently with a man as sound and widely respected as Belikov, he frowned and muttered: 'It's not my business. Let her marry the viper. I don't choose to interfere in what's someone else's affair.'

Now listen to what came next. Some mischief-maker drew a caricature: Belikov was walking in his galoshes with hitched-up trousers and an umbrella, his arm around Varenka; underneath was the inscription: *'Anthropos in Love.'* His expression captured, you must understand, perfectly. The artist must have worked for days, since all the teachers of the boys' school and the girls' school, the teachers at the seminary, the school officials – all received a copy. Belikov

Belikov

received one too. The caricature had a very serious effect on him.

We were leaving our building together – it was on the very first day of May, a Sunday, and all of us, teachers and students, had arranged to meet at the school and afterwards go together on foot to a grove outside town. We were setting out, and he was looking quite green, his expression dark and clouded.

'How unpleasant they are, angry people,' he said, and his lips trembled.

He had become pitiable to me now. We're walking along together, and then, just imagine, Kovalenko rides past on a bicycle, and behind him Varenka, also on a bicycle, red-faced, breathless, but happy and cheerful.

'We're on our way,' she cries out. 'Such lovely weather, so lovely that it's simply scary.'

And they both passed out of sight. My Belikov had gone from green to white, as if frozen solid. He stopped and looked at me.

'If you'll permit me to ask, just what is all

this?' he said. 'Or perhaps my eyes deceive me. Is it really decent for a teacher or a woman to go about on a bicycle?'

'Just what isn't decent about it?' I said. 'Let them ride around to their hearts' content.'

'No, how can you?' he wailed, amazed at my tranquility. 'What are you saying?'

He was so stricken that he didn't want to go on any further and returned home.

The next day he couldn't stop nervously rubbing his hands, and wincing, and one could see on his face that he was unhappy. He left work early for the first time in his life. And he didn't eat dinner. During the evening he dressed himself very warmly, although outdoors it was still perfect summer weather, and he set out to Kovalenko's. Varenka wasn't home. Only her brother was there.

'I humbly beg you to sit down,' Kovalenko said coldly, a frown on his brow, his face sleepy. He'd been napping after dinner and was dozy and out of spirits.

Belikov sat in silence for ten minutes and then started to speak.

'I came to see you in order to relieve my mind. This is very, very hard for me. Some vengeful person drew myself and another person of high rank in a ridiculous manner, and intimately close together – but I consider it my duty to put my trust in you, and I am not here about all that . . . I gave no sort of cause for this ridicule – just the opposite, as I have always conducted myself as an entirely decent man.'

Kovalenko sat quietly sulking. Belikov waited for a little while and continued softly in a mournful voice.

'I have something else to say to you. I have been in the profession for a long time, but you are only just beginning your service, and I have been considering, as an older colleague, how to put you on your guard. You ride a bicycle, and this amusement is absolutely improper for a teacher of young people.'

'And just why?' asked Kovalenko in his deep voice.

'But really, does this still need an explanation, Mikhail Savvich, isn't it perfectly clear? If a teacher goes by bicycle, what about the students? The only thing left is to go upside down! Since yours is not a prescribed means of transport, it can't be accepted. Yesterday I was horrified. When I observed your younger sister my eyes grew clouded. A woman or a girl on a bicycle – it's terrible.'

'Just what exactly is it you want?'

'I would like just one thing – to put you on your guard, Mikhail Savvich. You're a young man, you have your future in front of you. You must behave yourself very, very carefully, and you are so careless, oh how careless. You go out in an embroidered shirt, always out in the street with your books, and now there's this bicycle. When the principal learns that you and your younger sister were riding bicycles, and when it reaches the trustee . . . what then?'

'That I and my sister ride bicycles is no-body's business,' Kovalenko said and grew red in the face. 'And anyone who goes about to inter-fere in my family and domestic affairs, well, he can go to the bitches of the devil.'

Belikov grew pale but did not move.

'If you speak to me in such a tone, then I can't go on,' he said. 'And I ask that you never express yourself in that way about your superiors in my presence. You ought to have due regard for authority.'

'And what if I say that your authority is evil?' Kovalenko asked, looking at him spite-fully. 'Please leave me in peace. I am an honest man, and I don't wish to converse with such gentlemen as you. I don't like tattletales.'

Belikov began to fidget nervously, then quickly began to dress himself, an expression of shock on his face. It was the first time in his life, you see, that he had heard such rude words.

'You may say whatever you like,' he said, starting out onto the stair landing. 'I must only give you notice that it may be someone has heard us, and in order that our conversation not be misunderstood and something come of it, I will feel it necessary to make a report to our gentleman principal of the content of our conversation ... the 'devils' in particular. I am bound to do so.'

'Make a report? Then go and report.'

Kovalenko seized him by the collar and pushed, and Belikov pitched down the stairs, his galoshes thumping. The stairs were high and steep, but he flew to the bottom unharmed, stopped and touched himself on the nose. Were his glasses safe? And just at that moment, as he was hurtling down the stairs, Varenka had come in and two ladies with her; they stood at the bottom of the stairs and watched – and for Belikov this was the most terrible thing of all. It would have been better, it seemed to him, to break his neck, both legs, than to become a laughingstock. Why now the whole city would know, it would reach the principal, the trustees

– oh if only he hadn't come – someone would draw a new caricature, and all of this would end up with an order for his dismissal . . .

As he straightened himself up, Varenka recognized him, and looking at his comical features, rumpled coat, galoshes, not understanding what was going on and supposing that he had fallen on his own, she couldn't control herself, and the whole house was filled with her laughter.

'Ha-ha-ha!'

And with this booming, overflowing *ha-ha-ha* it all came to an end, both the match-making and Belikov's earthly existence. He no longer heard what Varenka was saying, and he saw nothing. Returning to his own place, he first of all took her portrait off the table, and afterward he lay down and didn't get up again.

Three days later Aphanasy came to my door and asked if he shouldn't send for a doctor, since something was wrong with his master. I went to Belikov's apartment. He was lying behind the bed curtains, covered with a blanket, silent. You asked him a question and got only yes or no – and not another sound. He lay there and Aphanasy wandered about nearby, gloomy, frowning, sighing heavily, smelling of vodka like a tavern.

A month later Belikov died. We all went to his funeral, including all the students and the seminarians. As he lay in his coffin, his expression was gentle, contented, as if he was glad we'd finally laid him in a box from which he'd never again have to arise. Yes, he had reached his ideal! And as if in his honour, at the hour of his funeral the weather grew clouded, rainy; we were all in galoshes and carried umbrellas. Varenka too was in galoshes, and when they lowered the coffin into the grave, she shed a few tears. I have noticed that Ukrainian women only cry or laugh; nothing in-between exists for them.

I must confess that to bury someone like Belikov is a great pleasure. When we returned from the cemetery we all wore a humble, pious expression: no one wished to betray this feeling of pleasure – a feeling like that which we experienced long, long ago, back in childhood when the grown-ups left the house, and we ran to the garden the next second, revelling in our total freedom. Ah, freedom, freedom! Even a hint, even a faint hope of it, its very possibility, gives wings to the soul, isn't that so?

We came back from the cemetery in a good mood. But that went on no more than a week, and life flowed by just as before, harsh, dull, stupid life, nothing to stop it going round and round, everything unresolved; things didn't get better. And truly, we had buried Belikov, but how many such men still remained, enclosed in their shells, how many of them there will be, still."

"Yes, there you have it, the way it is," Ivan Ivanych said and lit up his pipe.

"How many of them there will be still," Burkin repeated.

The teacher came out of the shed. He was not a very tall man, stout, quite bald, with a dark beard almost to his belt. With him came the two dogs.

"Oh moon, moon," he said, looking upward.

It was already midnight. To the right the whole village was visible, the long street stretched into the distance for three miles. It was all immersed in a deep, quiet sleep; neither motion nor sound, it was hard to believe that nature could be so peaceful. When, on a moonlit night, you see a wide village street with its peasant houses, haystacks, sleeping willows, tranquility enters the soul; in this calm, wrapped in the shade of night, free from struggle, anxiety and passion, everything is gentle, wistful, beautiful, and it seems that the stars are watching over it tenderly and with love, and that this is taking place somewhere unearthly, and that all is well. On the left, at the edge of the village, the countryside began; it was visible for a long way, as far as the horizon, and to its full extent this open land was lit by moonlight, and there was neither movement nor sound.

"Yes, there you have it," repeated Ivan Ivanych. "And you know, the way we live in the city, the closeness, crowded together, how we sign unnecessary documents, play cards, isn't that really a shell? And the way we lead our whole lives among loafers, people pursuing lawsuits, fools, idle women, talking and listening to all manner of nonsense, isn't that really a shell? Look, if you like I'll tell you an interesting story."

"No, it's past time to sleep," Burkin said. "Tell me tomorrow."

They both went into the shed and lay down in the hay. And soon both covered themselves and dozed off until suddenly they heard a light step, *tup*, *tup* . . . Someone was walking not far from the shed, went a few steps, stopped, and in a minute, once again, *tup*, *tup* . . . The dogs stirred.

"That's Mavra walking past," Burkin said.

The steps died away.

"You watch and listen while they tell lies," pronounced Ivan Ivanych, turning on his other side, "and they call you a fool because you put up with the lies; you put up with injuries, humiliations, not daring to declare openly that you are on the side of the free, honest people, and you lie to yourself, you smile, and all this for the sake of a loaf of bread and warm coals, for the sake of a propriety that's not worth a penny – no, it's impossible to live any longer like this."

"Well, that's from another opera, Ivan Ivanych," the teacher said. "Let's go to sleep."

And after ten minutes Burkin was asleep. But Ivan Ivanych kept turning from side to side and sighing, and then he got up, went outside again, and sitting by the door, began to smoke his pipe.

# 2

# Gooseberries

Alyokhin

 ince early morning the whole sky had been overcast with rain clouds; it was still, but not warm and dreary like those dull grey days when clouds hang over the fields for such a long time while you wait for rain that doesn't come. Ivan Ivanych, the veterinarian, and Burkin, the teacher, had grown tired of walking, and the field in front of them appeared endless. Far ahead, scarcely visible, the windmills of the village of Mironositskoe stretched to their right, and then a row of low hills disappeared into the distance beyond the village; they were both familiar with the riverbank, the meadows, yellow willows, farmsteads; if one stood on one of the little hills there was a view of the vast field, the telegraph, and the train, which came forth like a creeping caterpillar and in clear weather was visible all the way to the city. Now in calm weather when all nature seemed gentle and pensive, Ivan Ivanych and Burkin were inspired by love of this landscape, and both thought how grand and beautiful the country was.

"Before, when we were in the village elder's hut," Burkin said, "you had it in mind to tell some story."

"Yes, I wanted to tell about my brother."

Ivan Ivanych gave a deep sigh and lit his pipe, ready to begin telling his story, but just at that moment the rain came on. And within five minutes a heavy rain was pouring down on all sides, and it was hard to foresee when it might end. Ivan Ivanych and Burkin stood hesitating; the dogs, already soaked, put their tails between their legs and looked toward them pathetically.

"We have to find shelter somewhere," Burkin said. "Let's go to Alyokhin's. It's close by."

"Let's go."

They turned aside and walked steadily through the mown fields, first straight on, then bearing right until they reached the road. Soon poplars came into sight, an orchard, then the red roofs of the barns; a river shone and the view opened out on a wide pool with a mill and a white bathhouse. This was Sophina, where Alyokhin lived.

The mill was working, drowning out the sound of the rain; the dam trembled. By the wagons stood wet horses, hanging their heads, and people went back and forth, covering themselves with sacks. It was damp, muddy, comfortless, and the pool looked cold and dire. Ivan

Ivanych and Burkin experienced a sensation of wetness and dirt, a discomfort through the whole body, feet heavy with mud, and as they crossed the dam to climb toward the manorial barns, they were silent, as if angry with one another.

In one of the barns a winnowing machine was noisily at work; the door was open, and dust poured out. Just at hand stood Alyokhin himself, a man of forty, tall, heavy, with long hair, more like a professor or artist than a landowner. He wore a white but long-unwashed shirt with a rope belt, long johns instead of trousers, and his boots were clotted with mud and straw. His nose and eyes were black with dust. He recognized Ivan Ivanych and Burkin, and it was obvious he was glad to see them.

"To the house, please, gentlemen," he said, smiling. "I'll be there right away, this very minute."

The house was large, with two storeys. Alyokhin lived downstairs in two rooms with vaulted ceilings and small windows, where the farm managers used to live. The furnishings were simple, and it smelled of rye bread, cheap vodka, and harness. He seldom went upstairs to the reception rooms, only when guests arrived. A maid welcomed Burkin and Ivan Ivanych to the house, a young woman so beautiful that they both stopped short and stared at each other.

"You can't imagine how glad I am to see you, gentlemen," Alyokhin said as he came into the antechamber behind them. "I certainly didn't expect you." He turned to the maid. "Pelageya, offer our guests someplace to change their clothes. Yes, and while you do, I'll change mine. Only first I must go and wash up; it must look as if I haven't washed since spring. Come to the bathhouse if you like, by then they'll have everything here prepared."

The beautiful Pelageya, so tactful, so pleasing to look at, brought soap and towelling, and Alyokhin went to the bathhouse with his guests.

"Yes it's been a good while since I washed," he said, as he undressed. "My bathhouse, as you see, is a fine one, my father built it long since, but somehow it never gets used."

He sat on the step and soaped his long hair and his neck, and the water around him turned brown.

"Yes, I can see . . . ," pronounced Ivan Ivanych, glancing meaningfully at his head.

"Haven't washed for a long time now," Alyokhin repeated self-consciously, and soaped himself again, and the water around him turned dark blue, almost black.

Ivan Ivanych went outside, plunged into the water with a splash and started swimming along under the rain, stretching his arms wide, and waves spread outward, and the white water-lilies rocked on the waves; he swam out to the very centre of the pool and dived, and after a moment he appeared in another place, and began to swim further, diving over and over, trying to reach the bottom. "Oh my God . . . ," he repeated delightedly. "Oh my God . . ." He swam over to the mill, and there he talked about something with the men, then turned back and lay in the centre of the pool, turning his face up under the rain. Burkin and Alyokhin, dressed again, were prepared to leave, but he continued to swim and dive.

"Oh my God," he said, "Lord have mercy."

"So be it," Burkin shouted to him.

They returned to the house. And only when they had lit the lamp in the big sitting room upstairs, and Burkin and Ivan Ivanych, dressed in silk dressing gowns and warm slippers, were sitting in armchairs, and Alyokhin himself, washed, his hair brushed, in a new frock coat, had come to the sitting room, visibly pleased at feeling the warmth, clean, dry clothes, comfortable footwear, and after the beautiful Pelageya, her footsteps noiseless on the carpet, had brought a tray of tea and jam, only then did Ivan Ivanych begin his story, and it seemed that not only Burkin and Alyokhin were listening to him but also the old and young ladies and the soldiers quietly and severely observing from gold frames.

"We are two brothers," he began, "myself, Ivan Ivanych, and the other, Nikolai Ivanych, the younger by two years. I entered a course of study and became a veterinarian, while Nikolai, when he was nineteen, took up a position in the department of finance. Our father, Chimsha-Himalaiski, was a private's son, but by qualifying as an officer he left us with the rank and estate of gentlemen. After his death our inheritance was all tied up in debt, but whatever was to come later on, we passed our childhood in the country, doing as we pleased. Day and night we ran about the fields and the woods just like peasant children, guarding the horses, stripping bark off the lindens, catching fish, things like that ... And you know that anyone who at some time in his life has caught perch or watched the migrating thrushes, how they rush about in flocks over the countryside in the clear cool days, will never be a city boy, and until the day of his death will savour such liberty. My brother was miserable in the finance department. The years passed, and he sat there, always in one place, always writing on the same paper and always thinking just one thing – if only he was in the country. And this yearning of his turned little by little into a settled wish, a dream of buying himself a little country place, somewhere on the shore of a lake or river.

He was a good, humble man, I loved him, but I never sympathized with the way he imprisoned himself all his life in this wish to own a place in the country. There's a saying that a man needs only six feet of land. But of course the six feet is what you need for a corpse, not a man. These days they say that it's a fine thing when our educated men feel the pull of the land and aspire to a country estate. But this country estate comes down to the same six feet of earth. Leaving the city, the struggle, leaving the worldly clamour in order to hide away at a place

in the country, that isn't life, that's egotism, idleness, it's some kind of monasticism, but monasticism without the challenges. A man doesn't need six feet of earth, or a place in the country, but the whole globe, the whole of nature, where there's scope to manifest all that he is, all the qualities of his free soul.

My brother Nikolai, sitting at home in his study, dreamed of how he would eat cabbage soup from his own land, how the appetizing smell would fill the whole yard, and he'd eat on the green grass, sleep in the sun, sit for whole hours outside the gate on a little bench and look at the fields and woods.

Pamphlets on agriculture and the kind of advice found in almanacs gave shape to his enjoyment, were his favourite spiritual food; he loved to read newspapers, but in them he read only the one thing, advertisements for the sale of so many tenths of ploughed land and meadow, with a farmhouse, a river, an orchard, a mill with spring-fed ponds. And there loomed up in his head paths in the garden, flowers, fruit, houses for starlings, carp in the ponds, you know, all that stuff. These imaginary pictures changed, depending on the advertisement he'd come across, but for some reason, in every one, without fail, there were gooseberries. He could fancy no farm, no poetic nook, without gooseberries.

'Country life has its comforts,' he used to say. 'Sitting out on the balcony you drink your tea, and the ducks float on the pond, it smells so good . . . and the gooseberries are growing.'

He'd draw a plan of his estate, and every time on his plan appeared the same a) gentleman's house, b) servants' quarters, c) vegetable garden, d) gooseberries. He lived on the cheap: he was underfed, he didn't drink, he dressed God knows how, like a beggar, and everything was saved up and put in the bank. He was terribly stingy. It made me sick to look at him, and I'd give him something or send holiday gifts, and he hid it all away.

Once a man gives himself up to an idea there's nothing you can do.

Years passed, he was sent to another province, past forty by now, and he still read those advertisements in the newspapers and went on saving. Then I heard he got married. For one simple reason, to buy his country place with the gooseberries, he married an old and unattractive widow with no family, and only because she came with a bit of money. He lived on the cheap with her too, kept her hungry, and her money was put in the bank in his name. Before this, she had lived with the postmaster and with him was accustomed to pies and brandies, but with her second husband she didn't see even black bread in any abundance; as a result of that kind of life she began to waste away; she endured three years then gave up her soul to God. And of course my brother didn't think for a moment that he was to blame for her death. Money's like vodka, it can make a man strange. Among us in the city a merchant died. Just before his death he demanded a plate of honey and ate all his cash and his lottery tickets along with the honey, so nobody could get at them. Sometimes I examine cattle at the railway station, and one time a young gentleman fell under a locomotive, and it cut off his leg. We took him into the waiting room, blood flying around – a terrible thing, and there he is, frantic, asking if they've found his leg; in the boot on the leg that's been cut off is twenty roubles and he doesn't want them to be lost."

"But that's from another opera," Burkin said.

"After the death of his wife," Ivan Ivanych continued after a moment's thought, "my brother began to look around for an estate. Of course even if you search for five years, in the end you can still get it wrong, and buy something that's not at all what you dreamed of. Through a broker and with a mortgage transfer my brother Nikolai bought a hundred and twenty tenths, with a gentleman's house,

Nikolai Ivanych

servants' quarters, a park, but neither an orchard nor gooseberries, nor a pond with ducks; there was a river, but the water in it was the colour of coffee because on one side of the property was a brickworks, and on the other a glue factory. But my Nikolai Ivanych didn't gripe; he ordered himself twenty gooseberry bushes, planted them and settled in as lord of the manor.

The next year I went to see him. Travel there, think, observe how things are going on. In his letters my brother called his estate *The Chumbaroklov Wasteland, now Himalaiskoe.* I arrived at this *now Himalaiskoe* after noon. It was hot. Everywhere ditches, fences, hedges, barriers, tool handles, rows of fir trees – and I can't figure out how to get into the yard or where to tie my horse. I walk toward the house, and there to meet me is a red-coloured dog, fat and looking like a pig. He wants to bark, but he's too lazy. Out of the house came the cook, bare-legged, fat, also looking like a pig, and she said that the gentleman was taking a nap after lunch. I go in to my brother, he's sitting in bed, his knees covered with a blanket; he's aged, got fat, flabby, his cheeks, nose and lips bulging – looks as if he'll give a grunt under the blanket.

We embraced and shed a few tears, out of gladness and the sad thought that once we were young and now were both grey-haired and soon enough to die. He dressed and took me out to show me his estate.

'Well, and how is life going for you here?' I asked.

'Not bad at all. I swear to God I live happily.'

This was no longer the poor timid devil of a functionary, but the present-day landowner, a gentleman. He'd already made himself at home here, settled in and starting to enjoy it all; he ate a lot, soaped himself in the bathhouse, put on weight, had gone to law against the community and both factories, and he took great offense when the peasants didn't call him 'Your Excellency.' He dealt with spiritual matters firmly, in the grand manner, and he performed his acts of charity, not simply but with a flourish. What acts of charity? He treated the peasants for every illness with soda and castor oil, and on the afternoon of his name day he offered public prayers in the middle of the village and afterwards he set out a gallon of vodka as he thought he should. Oh those terrible gallons of vodka! Today a fat landowner drags the peasants to an assembly to account for the crop damage by their cattle, and tomorrow, on a festival day, he stands them a full gallon, and they drink and shout 'Hurray,' and drunk, they bow at his feet. A change for the better in his life, a full stomach and idleness, create a self-importance in a Russian, a towering insolence. Nikolai Ivanych, a clerk in the finance department afraid even to see with his own eyes, now spoke only truisms in the tone of a cabinet minister: 'Education is necessary, but for the people it is premature,' 'Corporal punishment is harmful in general, but in some cases it is wholesome and indispensible.'

'I know the people and am able to deal with them,' he said. 'The people love me. I have only to wave a finger, and the people will do anything I wish.'

And all this, of course, is said with a wise, kindly smile. He repeated twenty times, 'we of the gentry,' 'I as a gentleman': obviously he didn't remember that our grandfather was a peasant and our father only a soldier. Even our family name, Chimsha-Himalaiski, absurd as it is, seemed to him sonorous, distinguished and very pleasing.

But what I have to say is not about him, but about me. I want to tell you the change that took place in me during those few hours when I was at his country estate. In the evening, when we were drinking tea, the cook put on the table a whole plate of gooseberries. These were not bought but home grown, the first gathered since the bushes were planted. Nikolai Ivanych laughed, then for a moment he stared silently at the gooseberries, tears in his eyes – he couldn't speak for emotion – then he placed one berry in his mouth, gazed at me with the solemnity of a child who has at last received a toy he's set his heart on, and he said: 'How delicious!'

And he ate it greedily and said over again:

'Oh how delicious. You try one.'

It was hard and sour, but as Pushkin said, 'Deception that exalts is dearer than thousands of truths.' I saw a happy man, whose cherished dream had come true, who had achieved his goal in life, received what he wished for, who was contented with his country estate, with what he had become. To me, for some reason, the idea of human happiness is always tinged with melancholy, and right now at the sight of a happy man I was oppressed, felt something like despair. As usual I was depressed in the night. They made up a bed for me in a room next to my brother's bedroom, and I could hear that he didn't sleep, how he got up and went to the plate of gooseberries and took some. I pondered it, how many people are by and large happy and contented. What an overpowering force that is! Take a look at our life: the insolence, effrontery and idleness of the strong, the ignorance and animal squalor of the weak – all around uncontrolled poverty, narrowness, degeneracy, drunkenness, hypocrisy, lies . . . Meanwhile in every home and on the streets, peace, tranquility; out of fifty thousand living in the city not one to cry out, grow loud and indignant. We see them shop for groceries, eat by day, sleep at night, talk their nonsense, get married, grow old, complacently drag their deceased to the churchyard; but we don't see and don't hear what they suffer, the terrible things that take place behind the scenes. Everything is peaceful, calm, and only certain mute statistics protest: how many lose their minds, how many drink by the gallon, how many children die of hunger . . . The order of things is what it must be; it's obvious that the happy man feels good only because the unhappy carry their burden in silence, and without this silence happiness would be impossible. We're in a hypnotic trance. What do we need? Someone to stand with a little hammer at the door of every satisfied, happy man, the tapping a constant reminder that the unhappy exist, that though he may be happy, life will sooner or later show him its claws, misfortune befall him – sickness, poverty, loss, and no one will see or hear, as now he doesn't see or hear the others. But there is no man with a little hammer; the happy man lives for himself with only small worldly anxieties to disturb him a little, like wind in the aspens – and all goes well.

That night it was clear to me that I too was contented, complacent," Ivan Ivanych continued, standing up. "After dinner or out hunting, I too have sermonized about how to live, what to believe in, how to govern the nation. I too have declared what's to be taught to the world, how education is necessary, but for the simple people it is enough to read and write. Freedom is a blessing, I've said, without it there is nothing, it's like being without air, but for now it's necessary to wait. Yes, I've said that, and now I'm asking, Wait in whose name?" As Ivan Ivanych spoke he looked angrily at Burkin. "Wait in whose name? I ask you that. And for what reason? They say to me, Not all at once, every idea comes to fruition gradually, in its own time. But who says this? Where are the proofs that this is just? You refer to the natural order of things, to the laws of phenomena, but is there order and law in this, that I stand aside and wait, a living, thinking man, stand above a ditch and wait while it is collapsing or sinking into the silt at a moment when I could leap across it or build a bridge over it? I say yet again, Wait in whose name? To wait when there is no strength to live, but nevertheless a duty to live and a will to live.

I left my brother early in the morning, and since then it's become unbearable to be in the city. The peace and tranquility oppress me. I'm afraid to look into a window since there is no sight more painful to me now than a happy family sitting around a table and drinking tea. I'm already old and unfit for the struggle, I'm not even capable of hate. Only I grieve, I'm vexed and sore, in the night my head's on fire with the rush of thoughts, and I can't sleep . . . Oh if only I were young."

In his agitation, Ivan Ivanych propelled himself from one corner to another and repeated, "If only I were young."

He suddenly went up to Alyokhin and began to shake first his one hand then the other.

"Pavel Konstantinovich," he went on in an entreating voice, "don't settle down, don't let yourself be lulled to sleep. While you're young and powerful and brisk, don't weary in doing good. Happiness is nothing, inessential; if there is a reason, a purpose to life, that reason and purpose is not to aim at happiness, but something higher and wiser. Do good."

All this Ivan Ivanych spoke with a pitiable, beseeching smile, as if he was begging a favour for himself.

Then all three sat in their armchairs, in different corners of the sitting room and were silent. Ivan Ivanych's story didn't satisfy either Burkin or Alyokhin. As the generals and ladies watched from the gold frames, seeming to be alive in the twilight, listening to a story about a poor devil of a clerk who ate gooseberries was boring. They would have liked some sort of conversation about people of refinement, about women. And the fact that they were sitting in a drawing room where everything – chandeliers in slipcovers, armchairs, carpets under foot – spoke of how at one time those very same people who watched from the frames had walked here, sat, taken tea where now the beautiful Pelageya moved about so silently – this was better than any such stories.

Alyokhin badly wanted to go to sleep; he had started in at the farm work early, at three o'clock in the morning, and now his eyes were closing, but he was afraid that his guests might discuss something interesting without him, and he didn't want that. He didn't try to grasp whether what Ivan Ivanych had said was wise or just; that the guests didn't discuss grain or hay or tar but things that had no direct connection to his life pleased him, and he wanted them to go on . . .

"Well I'm ready to sleep," Burkin, said as he stood up. "Let me wish you a good night."

Alyokhin took his leave, went off to his room downstairs, and his guests stayed above. A large room was allocated to the two of them for the night, and in it stood two wooden bedsteads with ornamental carvings, and in a corner was an ivory crucifix; each of their beds was wide, freshly made by the beautiful Pelageya, smelling pleasantly of clean linen.

Ivan Ivanych undressed in silence and lay down.

"Lord, pardon us sinners," he said and pulled the covers over his head.

From his pipe lying on the table there was a strong smell of burnt tobacco, and for a long time Burkin couldn't sleep but couldn't understand where the strong smell was coming from.

The rain beat against the windows all night.

# 3

# About Love

The Beautiful Pelageya

The next day they were served some delicious meat turnovers, crayfish, and lamb cutlets for lunch, and while they were eating, Nikanor the cook came upstairs to ask what the guests wanted for dinner. This Nikanor was a man of medium height with a pudgy face and little eyes, clean-shaven, with a moustache that looked not so much shaved as plucked out.

Alyokhin had told them that the beautiful Pelageya was in love with this cook. Since he was a drinker with a violent temper, she didn't want to marry him, but offered to live with him all the same. But he was very pious, and his religious principles wouldn't allow him to live like that. He insisted that she marry him – he would have nothing else – and when he was drinking he berated her, even hit her. When he was drinking she hid in the upstairs, sobbing, and then Alyokhin and his housekeeper wouldn't leave the place so they could defend her if that was necessary.

They began to talk about love.

"How love comes into being," Alyokhin said, "why Pelageya didn't fall in love with somebody more suitable for her with her inward and outward qualities, but instead chose to love that mug Nikanor" – everyone called him the ugly mug – "since what matters in love is personal happiness, it's beyond all knowing, say what you like about it. Up till now we have only this irrefutable truth about love – 'It's a sheer, utter mystery,' – every other single thing that has been said or written about it is not an answer but a reframing of the question, which remains unresolved. The explanation which would seem to be right for one case isn't right for ten others, so what's much the best, in my judgment, is to explain each case separately, not attempting to generalize. What we need, as the doctors say, is to individualize each separate case."

"Absolutely right," Burkin agreed.

"We respectable Russians nourish a predilection for such questions, but we have no answers. Ordinarily love is poeticized, adorned with roses and nightingales, but we Russians have to dress up our love with disastrous questions. Chances are we'll pick out the most uninteresting. In Moscow when I was still a student I had a girl in my life, sweet, ladylike, but every time I took her in my arms, she thought about what monthly allowance I'd give her and what a pound of suet cost that day. Really! And when we're in love we don't stop asking ourselves these questions: sincere or insincere, wise or foolish, what our love is revealing, and so on and on. Whether this is good or bad I don't know, what it gets in the way of, fails to satisfy, irritates, I just don't know."

It was like this when he had something he wanted to talk about. With people living alone there was always some such thing in their thoughts, something they were eager to say. In the city bachelors went to the baths or the restaurants on purpose just so they could chat or sometimes tell their so-interesting stories to the attendants or the waiters, and then in the country they habitually poured out their thoughts to their guests. At that moment all you could see outside the window was a grey sky and trees wet with rain; in this weather there was no place to go and nothing remained but to tell stories and listen to them.

"I've been living at Sophina and busy with the farm for a long time now," began Alyokhin, "ever since I finished university. By education

I'm a gentleman, by inclination a thinking man, but when I arrived here at the estate, it carried a big debt, since my father had borrowed money, partly because he spent a lot on my education, so I decided not to leave here, but to work until I paid off the debt. I made the decision and started in to work, not, I confess, without a certain repugnance. The land here doesn't produce much, and for agriculture not to be a losing proposition it's necessary to profit by the labour of serfs – or hired hands which is about the same thing – or to farm in the peasant way, which means working in the fields yourself alongside your family. There's no middle way here. But I didn't shilly-shally. I didn't leave a scrap of land untouched. I dragged in every peasant man and woman from the neighbouring villages; work here was always at a raging boil. Myself, I ploughed, sowed, cut the grain; when I grew bored I wrinkled up my face like a farm cat who's eaten cucumber from the vegetable garden. My body ached and I slept on my feet.

At the beginning it seemed to me that I could easily reconcile this labouring life with my educated habits – all that counts, I thought, is to behave with a certain outward order. I settled upstairs here in these splendid reception rooms, and I curtained them off so that after lunch or dinner I was served coffee and liqueurs, and at night while I was lying down to sleep I read the *European Herald.* But one day our priest arrived, Father Ivan, and he drank all the liqueurs at one go, and the *European Herald* went to the priest's daughters. In summer, especially during haymaking, I didn't have time to get to my own bed, I'd take cover in a shed, on a stone boat, or somewhere in a forester's hut – but why go on about it? Little by little I moved downstairs, I began to eat in the servants' kitchen; all that remained to me from our former luxury was the servants who had worked for my father, and to discharge them would have been painful.

In those first years here I was appointed honorary justice of the peace. Whenever I had occasion to go into the city, I'd take part in the session of the district law court; it was a diversion for me. When you go on here without a break for two or three months, especially in the winter, in the end you get to pining for your black frock coat. And at the district court there were frock coats and full dress coats and tail coats, and there were lawyers, men who'd received the standard education: I'd get into conversation with them. After sleeping on a stone boat, after sitting in a chair in the servants' kitchen, to be in clean linen, light boots, with a chain on my breast – this was real luxury!

In the city they received me amicably. I was ready to make acquaintances, and out of them all, the soundest, and to tell the truth the pleasantest for me, was a friendly connection with Luganovich, the cordial Chairman of the district court. An attractive personality: you both know him. This was right after the famous affair of the arsonists; the trial lasted two days, we were tired out. Luganovich looked at me and he said, 'You know what? You should come to dinner.'

This was unexpected since beside Luganovich I was of little significance, just some functionary, and I had never been at his home. I stopped off in my room for just a moment to change my clothes, and we set off for dinner. And there the opportunity presented itself to make the acquaintance of Anna Alexeyevna, Luganovich's wife. She was still very young then, not more than 22 years old, and half a year later she was to have her first child. The past is past, and right now I'd find it difficult to define exactly what it was about her that was unusual, what it was in her I liked so much, but over dinner everything was irresistibly fine. I saw a young woman, beautiful, good, cultured, charming, a woman I'd never met, and right away I felt a sensation of familiarity, as if I'd seen her before – that face, those clever, friendly eyes – in an album that lay on my mother's dresser.

In the arson case we'd prosecuted four Jews, supposed to be a criminal gang, but as far as I could see, quite groundlessly. At dinner, I got very worked up, finding it all painful, I don't remember now what I said, only when I spoke Anna Alexeyevna turned her head and said to her husband, 'What is all this, Dmitri?'

Luganovich, that good soul, was one of those ingenuous men who hold firmly to the opinion that if a man is brought to court it means he's guilty, and that to question the rightness of a sentence may only be done by legitimate procedures on paper and certainly not over dinner and in a private conversation.

'We weren't on hand with them to set the fire,' he said softly, 'and we're not in court here to see them sentenced to prison.'

And both of them, husband and wife, did their best to get me to eat and drink a little more. By small things – this, for example, that they made coffee together, and this, how they understood each other in a flash – I could grasp

that they lived comfortably, in harmony, and that they were glad to have a guest. After dinner they played piano four hands, then later on it grew dark and I set off home. That was at the beginning of spring. Subsequently I passed the whole summer at Sophina, without a break, and there was not a moment for a passing thought about the city, but the memory of the well-proportioned, fair-haired woman stayed with me all day; I didn't think about her, but truly, her sweet shadow lay on my soul.

In the late fall there was a charity performance in the city. I entered the governor's loge – I was invited there during the intermission – and I saw, down the row with the governor's party, Anna Alexeyevna – once again, irresistibly, the intense impression of beauty, and the sweet, tender eyes, once again the sense of closeness.

We were seated side by side, then we started out to the foyer.

'You're losing weight,' she said, 'are you sick?'

'Yes. I've caught a chill in my shoulder, and in the rainy weather I have trouble sleeping.'

'You have a dull look about you. In the spring when you came to dinner, you were younger, more cheerful. In those days you were enthusiastic, always talking, you were very interesting, and I confess I was even a tiny bit taken with you. Often, as the year went by, you came to mind for some reason, and today when I was getting ready for the theatre it seemed to me that I'd see you.'

And she laughed.

'But today you have that dull look,' she repeated. 'It ages you.'

The next day I had lunch at the Luganovichs'. After lunch they left the house to go out to their summer place to put things in order for the winter, and I with them. And with them I returned to the city, and at midnight I drank tea in the quietness of their house, their domestic surroundings, as the fireplace burned, and the young mother kept going out of the room to see if her daughter was asleep. And after that with each arrival I found myself, without fail, at the Luganovich house. They expected it of me, and it was my habit. Usually I entered without being announced, like someone who lived there.

'Who is it?' I heard from a distant room the drawling voice that seemed to me so beautiful.

'It's Pavel Konstantinich,' answered the housemaid or the nurse.

Anna Alexeyevna came out to me with a worried look, and every time she asked, 'Why have you been away so long? Has something happened?'

Her glance, the fine, graceful hands which she reached out to me, her everyday clothes, the way she did her hair, the voice, her step, each time all of this produced an impression of something new, something extraordinary in my life, and important. We talked for hours and we were silent for hours, each thinking our own thoughts, or she played the piano for me. If no one was at home, I stayed on and waited, chatted with the nurse, played with the baby, or I lay in the study on the Turkish divan and read the newspaper, and when Anna Alexeyevna returned, I greeted her as she came in, took from her all her shopping, and for some reason, each time I took the shopping it was with as much love and exultation as a young boy.

There is a proverb: if an old woman has no problems, she'll buy a piglet. The Luganovichs had no problems so they made friends with me. If I didn't go to town for a while, it must mean I was sick or something had happened to me, and both of them grew terribly anxious. They worried that I, an educated person who knew languages, lived in the country instead of occupying myself with science or serious literary work, went round like a squirrel in a cage, worked a lot but never had a penny. To them it seemed that I must be suffering, and if I chatted, appeared confident, ate well, it must be an

Alyokhin & Anna Alexeyevna

attempt at concealing my suffering, and even in happy moments, when everything was fine with me, I had the sense of their searching looks. They were especially full of concern when I was actually having a hard time of it, when one creditor or another oppressed me or when money was insufficient for the payments demanded; husband and wife whispered together by the window, and in a while he'd come up to me and say, with a serious look, 'Pavel Konstantinich, if at present you should be in need of money, then my wife and I beg you not to feel shy, but to apply to us.'

And his ears grew red with embarrassment. That's just how it would happen, the whispering by the window and he would come toward me with red ears and say, 'My wife and I beg you earnestly to accept this present from us.'

Then he gave me some cufflinks, a cigarette case, or a lamp; and in response to this I would send from the country a dressed fowl, butter, flowers. It's to the point to say that both of them were well-to-do. From the first I had borrowed money and wasn't especially fastidious, borrowed where I could, but no power on earth would make me borrow from the Luganovichs. That's all there is to be said about that!

I was wretched. At home in the field or in a shed I thought about her, and I tried to see through the mystery of this young, beautiful, intelligent woman married to an uninteresting man, almost old – the husband was over forty – and bearing his children. How to understand the mystery of this uninteresting man, a good soul, a simple heart, who deliberated with such boring sobriety at balls and evening parties, took his place among responsible people, listless, superfluous, with a humble, apathetic expression, as if they might have brought him there for sale, who all the same believed in his right to be contented, to have children with her, and I struggled to understand why she was his and not mine, and why it must be that such a terrible mistake ruled our lives.

Arriving in the city, I saw in her eyes each time that she had been waiting for me; she herself confessed to me that whenever she perceived something unusual outside her window she guessed that I was arriving. We talked for hours or were silent, but we didn't confess to each other that we were in love; shyly, jealously, we dissembled. We were afraid of anything that might reveal our secret, even to ourselves. I loved her tenderly, deeply, but I debated, questioned myself about what our love might lead to if our strength wasn't sufficient for the battle against it; it seemed to me incredible that this calm melancholy love of mine might suddenly tear apart the happy, pleasing course of life of her husband and children, of everything in that house where they loved and trusted me so. Was this a decent thing to do? She might come to me, but where? Where could I take her away? It would be another thing altogether if mine were a pleasant, interesting life, if for example I were struggling to emancipate my native land, were a famous scholar, artist, painter, but no, I would carry her out of an ordinary, dull condition to another much the same, or to something even more humdrum. And how long would our happiness last? What would happen to her in case of my illness, death, or if we should simply stop loving each other?

And she, apparently, was having the same thoughts. She considered her husband, her children, her mother who loved the husband like a son. If she should give herself up to her feelings, then she would have to tell lies about her state or to speak the truth, and either one would be awkward and horrible. And this question tormented her: should she offer me happiness, her love, or not further complicate my life, already difficult, full of every kind of unhappiness? It seemed to her that she was already insufficiently youthful for me, insufficiently industrious and energetic to start a new life; she often talked to her husband about it – how I needed to marry a clever, worthy girl who would be a good housewife, a helper – and at once added that such a girl could hardly be found in the whole city.

Meanwhile the years passed. Anna Alexeyevna now had two children. When I arrived at the Luganovichs' the maid smiled pleasantly, the children shouted that Uncle Pavel Konstantinich had arrived and wrapped their arms round my neck, and everyone was happy. They didn't understand what was going on in my soul, and they thought that I too was happy. They all saw in me a noble being. Both the adults and the children felt that some noble being had entered the room and this induced in them an attitude of particular delight with me, as if in my presence their life was finer and more pleasant. Anna Alexeyevna and I went to the theatre together, always on foot; we sat in the row of chairs with our shoulders touching. In silence I took from her hand the opera glasses, and at that moment I sensed her closeness to me, that she was mine, and each of us was nothing without the other – yet by some strange misunderstanding, leaving the theatre we would each time say farewell and separate like strangers. What people in the city said about us, God knows, but in all they said there was not one word of the truth.

In the following years Anna Alexeyevna began to go away more often to visit her mother or her sister; bad moods came over her, a sense that her life was wrong, tainted, and then she didn't want to see either her husband or her children. By now she was receiving treatment for a nervous disorder.

We were silent, everyone was silent, but in the presence of strangers she experienced some odd irritation with me; she would disagree with whatever I said, and if I raised a question she would take the side of my opponent. When I dropped something she would say coldly, 'Congratulations.'

If, having gone to the theatre with her, I forgot to take the opera glasses, she would say, 'I knew you'd forget.'

Fortunately or unfortunately, nothing happens in our lives that doesn't end sooner or later. A time of separation came about when Luganovich was appointed Chairman in one of the western provinces. They had to sell furniture, horses, the summer place. When they went out to the cottage and back, looked around for a final time, looked at the garden, the green roof, it was sad for everyone, and I understood that the time had come to say goodbye, and not just to the cottage. It was decided that at the end of August we would see Anna Alexeyevna off to the Crimea, where her doctors were sending her, and a little later Luganovich would leave with the children for his western province.

We sent Anna Alexeyevna off, in a great crowd. When she had said goodbye to her husband and children, and there remained only an instant before the third bell, I came running toward her in her compartment in order to set on a shelf something from her work basket that she had almost forgotten; and we had to say goodbye. When our glances met, there in the compartment, strength of mind abandoned us both, I held her in my arms, she pressed her face to my chest, and tears flowed from her eyes; I kissed her face, shoulders, hands, all wet with tears – oh how unhappy we were about it! I confessed my love for her, and with a burning pain in my heart I understood how superfluous and small and illusory everything was that prevented us from loving. I understood that when you love, and when you think about this love, you must proceed from something higher, of more importance than happiness or unhappiness, sin or virtue in the commonplace sense; or you mustn't think about it at all.

I kissed her for the last time, shook her hand, and we separated – forever. The train was already moving. I sat down in the neighbouring compartment – it was empty – and until the first village I sat there and cried. Then I went on foot to my place at Sophina . . ."

While Alyokhin was telling his story the rain ended, and the sun came out. Burkin and Ivan Ivanych went out on the balcony; from it there was an attractive view of the garden and the stretch of river, which now shone in the sun like a mirror. They looked with admiration and at that moment felt sorry that the man with kind, wise eyes who talked to them with such candour, who really did go round and round on this huge estate like a squirrel in a cage, hadn't taken up science or some such thing which would make his life more pleasant; and they thought how sad her face must have been, the young lady, when he said goodbye to her in that compartment and kissed her face and shoulders. Both of them had run across her in the city, and Burkin had already made her acquaintance and found her attractive.

*Postscript*

Anton Chekhov spent the winter of 1897-98 in France, most of it in Nice on the Côte d'Azur. He was avoiding the cold and damp of the Russian winter. In March of 1897 he had suffered a severe haemorrhage and was told that both his lungs were tubercular. Though he himself was a doctor, he had for the previous ten years succeeded in ignoring the symptoms of his disease. Now he could no longer pretend not to understand the dangerous state of his health.

That winter Chekhov read extensively in French and was much impressed by Émile Zola's public intervention in the Dreyfus scandal.

(One suspects that the little anecdote in "About Love" concerning the supposed Jewish gangsters might have its origins in this.) Chekhov improved his knowledge of the French language – he was interviewed about the Dreyfus affair in French – but he did only a limited amount of writing. In May of 1898 he returned to his estate at Melikhovo, and in July and August he published in the magazine *Russian Thought* the three connected stories translated here. A year later he described them as a series still far from complete, but he never returned to them, and they appear to be his only experiment in linking his stories.

Within an overall narrative about the travels in the Russian countryside of the veterinarian Ivan Ivanych and the teacher Burkin, Chekhov presents three framed tales, the first a kind of grotesque comedy of the sort associated with Gogol, the second not dissimilar but with a more explicit and impassioned response from its narrator, the third a poignant little story of

failed love that may evoke for the reader
Chekhov's most famous story, "The Lady with a
Little Dog." Emotion grows more personal as
we move from one to the next. In the first story
Burkin tells a tale about an acquaintance. In the
second Ivan Ivanych describes the life of his
brother. In the third their friend Alyokhin
recounts a painful story about his own life.

While the framed tales provide the dramatic core of each story, the outer narrative
offers a vivid evocation of the Russian countryside, with a sense of history and geography
complementing and containing the urgency of
the tales. In "Gooseberries" an extraordinary
passage describes the aging veterinarian Ivan
Ivanych swimming in a cold mill pond, unwilling to stop, in the grip of some inexplicable
joy; then at a paragraph break the story modu-
lates in a single line to a quiet sitting room
where the framed portraits of soldiers and fine
ladies evoke a past gentility, and Ivan Ivanych
begins to talk about his brother's life, its

obsession, the coarse and joyless littleness of his achievement.

A passage from the conclusion of the first story lifts our gaze from the events we've just been told about. "When, on a moonlit night, you see a wide village street with its peasant houses, haystacks, sleeping willows, tranquility enters the soul; in this calm, wrapped in the shade of night, free from struggle, anxiety and passion, everything is gentle, wistful, beautiful, and it seems that the stars are watching over it tenderly and with love, and that this is taking place somewhere unearthly, and that all is well."

The point of view in Chekhov's stories can be slippery. The "you" of this passage is unidentified, but the verb is in the second person singular; it speaks intimately from some detached narrative intelligence to each single reader in a passage that evokes a benign universe surrounding the events.

Yet just a few lines earlier we have read Burkin's harsh conclusion to the tale he has been recounting. "We came back from the cemetery in a good mood. But that went on no more than a week, and life flowed by just as before, harsh, dull, stupid life, nothing to stop it going round and round, everything unresolved; things didn't get better."

Such a counterpoint of one voice with another, one mood with another, their contradiction, creates an ironic interplay not altogether unlike the form of Chekhov's plays. Always, in Chekhov, there is a sense that the events suggest numerous possibilities, things that could occur offstage or after the narrative ends. The very last line of "About Love," the third of these stories, offers a grim hint at what might be still to come.

In 1991 Oberon Press published *Last Stories*, my translations of the final six stories of Anton Chekhov's career, including two or three of his finest and best known works. It seems appropriate to repeat here what I said in the introduction to that book, that while there are many translators whose Russian is better than mine, there are not so many who have had a long experience of writing narrative prose. These narratives are my personal versions of Chekhov's stories; they are also as close as I can make them to the precision and suggestiveness of the originals.

This little book is homage to a great writer. It is dedicated to my two daughters, Maggie and Kate, who, many years ago, when I complained about the difficulty of finding Russian texts, collaborated to find and buy me a pile of second-hand books including the three volume collection of Chekhov stories from which the translations have been made.

**David Helwig** is the author of twenty volumes of fiction and fourteen volumes of poetry, an Officer of the Order of Canada, and former poet laureate of Prince Edward Island.

**Seth** is a cartoonist and designer. His books include, *George Sprott*, *Vernacular Drawings*, *Clyde Fans* and *It's a Good Life, If You Don't Weaken*. He has designed the *Portable Dorothy Parker*, *Make Way for Tomorrow* and *The Complete Peanuts*.

**Library and Archives Canada Cataloguing in Publication**

Chekhov, Anton Pavlovich, 1860-1904
About love : three stories / by Anton Chekhov ; translator,
David Helwig ; illustrator, Seth.

ISBN 978-1-926845-42-5

I. Helwig, David, 1938-  II. Seth, 1962-  III. Title.

PG3456.A15H44 2012      891.73'3      C2011-907873-2

PRINTED IN HONG KONG